D0573901

F   Bra

Brady, Jennifer

Jambi and the Lions

PROPERTY OF
ELMWOOD SCHOOLS
RHINELAND SCHOOL DIVISION #18

JAMBI AND THE LIONS

WRITTEN AND ILLUSTRATED BY JENNIFER BRADY

LANDMARK EDITIONS, INC.

P.O. Box 4469 • 1402 Kansas Avenue • Kansas City, Missouri 64127
(816) 241-4919

Dedicated to:
the protection of
all the world's animals.

COPYRIGHT © 1992 BY JENNIFER BRADY

International Standard Book Number: 0-933849-41-9 (LIB.BDG.)

Library of Congress Cataloging-in-Publication Data
Brady, Jennifer, 1973-
    Jambi and the lions / written and illustrated by Jennifer Brady.
        p.   cm.
    Summary: Jambi, a young Kenyan boy who has befriended a lion cub, tracks a band of poachers who have captured some of the lions in the cub's pride.
    ISBN 0-933849-41-9 (lib.bdg. : acid free)
    1. Youths' writings, American.
    [1. Lions—Fiction.   2. Kenya—Fiction.
    3. Poaching—Fiction.   4. Blacks—Kenya—Fiction.
    5. Youths' writings.

    I. Title.
    PZ7.B7293Jam   1992
    [Fic]—dc20   92-17593
                                                        CIP
                                                        AC

All rights reserved. Except for use in a review, neither all nor part of this publication may be reproduced, stored in a retrieval system, or transmitted in any form or by any means, electronic, mechanical photocopying, duplicating, recording or otherwise, without prior written permission of the publishers.

Editorial Coordinator: Nancy R. Thatch
Creative Coordinator: David Melton

Printed in the United States of America

Landmark Editions, Inc.
P.O. Box 4469
1402 Kansas Avenue
Kansas City, Missouri 64127
(816) 241-4919

The 1991 Panel of Judges

Richard F. Abrahamson, Ph.D.
    Director of Graduate Programs in
    Literature for Children and Adolescents
    University of Houston, TX
Kaye Anderson, Ph.D.
    Associate Professor, Teacher Education
    California State University at Long Beach
Teresa L. Barghoorn, Library Media Specialist (Retired)
    League City Intermediate School, League City, TX
Marge Hagerty Bergman, Library Media Specialist
    Educational Consultant, Landmark Editions, Inc.
Mary Jane Corbett, Library Media Specialist
    Chinn Elementary School, Kansas City, MO
Greg Denman, Writer and Storyteller
    Language Arts Consultant to Schools
Charlene F. Gaynor, Editor-in-Chief
    LEARNING '92
Kathy Henderson, Editor
    MARKET GUIDE FOR YOUNG WRITERS
Patricia B. Henry, National Chairperson Emeritus
    Young Authors' Days, International Reading Assn.
Bret-Alan Hubbard, Associate
    Landmark Editions, Inc.
Joan Dale Hubbard, Board Member
    The R.D. and Joan Dale Hubbard Foundation
Joyce E. Juntune, Executive Director
    American Creativity Association
Beverly Kelley, Library Media Specialist
    Crestview Elementary School, North Kansas City, MO
Jean Kern, Library Media Specialist
    President, Greater Kansas City
    Association of School Librarians
Joyce Leibold, Teacher (Retired)
    Chinn Elementary School, Kansas City, MO
Teresa M. Melton, Contest Director
    Landmark Editions, Inc.
John Micklos, Editor
    READING TODAY
Karen Orrill, Library Media Specialist
    Gracemor Elementary School, North Kansas City, MO
Dorothy Phoenix, Library Media Specialist (Retired)
    Indian Creek Elementary School, Kansas City, MO
Cathy Riggs-Salter
    Geography Consultant and Curriculum Developer
    The National Geographic Society
Shirley Ross, President Emeritus
    Missouri Association of School Librarians
Philip A. Sadler
    Associate Professor, Children's Literature
    Central Missouri State University
Nan Thatch, Editorial Coordinator
    Landmark Editions, Inc.
Kate Waters, Editor
    SCHOLASTIC Professional Books
Jane Y. Woodward, Editor
    CURRICULUM PRODUCT NEWS

Authors:
C.S. Adler — THE MISMATCHED SUMMER
Sandy Asher — WHERE DO YOU GET YOUR IDEAS?
Dana Brookins — ALONE IN WOLF HOLLOW
Clyde Robert Bulla — WHITE BIRD
Scott Corbett — WITCH HUNT
Julia Cunningham — OAF
Dorothy Francis — DRIFT BOTTLES IN HISTORY AND FOLKLORE
Jan Greenberg — THE PAINTER'S EYE: LEARNING TO
                LOOK AT CONTEMPORARY AMERICAN ART
Carol Kendall — THE GAMMAGE CUP
Lois Lowry — NUMBER THE STARS
Patricia R. Mauser — A BUNDLE OF STICKS
Kate McMullan — UNDER THE MUMMY'S SPELL
Hilary Milton — THE GITAWAY BOX
Willo Davis Roberts — JO AND THE BANDIT
Barbara Robinson — MY BROTHER LOUIS MEASURES WORMS
Theodore Taylor — THE HOSTAGE
Jane Resh Thomas — THE PRINCESS IN THE PIGPEN

Authors and Illustrators:
Michael Cain — THE LEGEND OF SIR MIGUEL
Aruna Chandrasekhar — OLIVER AND THE OIL SPILL
Stacy Chbosky — WHO OWNS THE SUN?
Amity Gaige — WE ARE A THUNDERSTORM
Lisa Gross — THE HALF & HALF DOG
Jonathan Kahn — PATULOUS, THE PRAIRIE RATTLESNAKE
Leslie Ann MacKeen — WHO CAN FIX IT?
David Melton — WRITTEN & ILLUSTRATED BY...
Jayna Miller — TOO MUCH TRICK OR TREAT
Adam Moore — BROKEN ARROW BOY
Lauren Peters — PROBLEMS AT THE NORTH POLE
Dav Pilkey — WORLD WAR WON
Cara Reichel — A STONE PROMISE
Anika Thomas — LIFE IN THE GHETTO

JAMBI AND THE LIONS

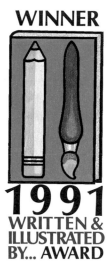

WINNER

1991
WRITTEN &
ILLUSTRATED
BY... AWARD

Landmark receives a lot of special interest books in THE NATIONAL WRITTEN & ILLUSTRATED BY... AWARDS CONTEST. We get dinosaur stories from kids who are fascinated with dinosaurs, unicorn stories from unicorn enthusiasts, and fluffy rabbit stories from fluffy rabbit fanciers.

Lions are definitely Jennifer Brady's special interest. She reads everything she can find on the subject — from Joy Adamson's BORN FREE to articles in NATIONAL GEOGRAPHIC magazines. She enjoys writing about lions. She likes to draw lions. And she loves to paint lions. So when she decided to create a book for the contest, her story had to be about... what else?... lions!

"In JAMBI AND THE LIONS," says Jennifer, "I wanted to tell a simple story about a Kenyan boy who cared so much about a pride of lions that in order to rescue them, he was willing to place his own life in danger. I wanted the illustrations to be beautiful and believable. I also hoped my book would inform young readers of the need to protect wild animals in their natural environments."

Jennifer has achieved all of her objectives in her beautifully written and illustrated book. You are now invited to experience that wonderful book, meet Jambi and the lions, and share the excitement of their African adventure.

— David Melton
Creative Coordinator
Landmark Editions, Inc.

JAMBI AND THE LIONS

Dawn's rays of golden sunlight poured over the savannah and warmed the valley with the brilliance of an African day. Thirsty gazelles gathered at the water hole, and zebras grazed on bush grass. Giraffes stretched their long necks to nibble tender leaves that grew at the tops of the acacia trees. Hoping for an easy kill, a lone cheetah circled and stalked an old wildebeest.

A pride of lions lazed about in the shade of one of the acacias. They dozed contentedly, their hunger satisfied by a meal of antelope from the night before.

When Jambi, a young Kenyan boy, appeared at the edge of the savannah, the lions paid little attention. They had grown accustomed to the native child who frequently watched them from the distance.

When Jambi took a few steps forward, only the large male lion slowly turned his head and looked intently at the boy. It was Koru, as Jambi called him, the king of the pride. The lion's stare was warning enough. Jambi knew better than to go any closer.

Without question Koru was the master and protector of the pride. He feared no animal, not even the other male lions that sometimes entered the savannah and tried to claim the territory. Only a few lions were brave enough to challenge Koru to a fight. None had ever won a battle against him.

This morning the pride rested peacefully, feeling safe under Koru's watchful eyes. Two old lionesses, Meta and Kiwi, napped at the fringe of shade cast by the acacia. Mara, a younger lioness, was stretched out near Koru, watching her year-old cubs, Kari and Pika, wrestle in the grass.

Kari was a curious little cub, but she was more timid than her brother Pika. Young Pika was mischievous and loved to stir up trouble. He frequently sneaked around, biting the tails of the other lions or suddenly pouncing on their backs.

When Pika became too rowdy, his mother would growl and give him a quick swat with her paw. Jambi admired Mara's strict, but gentle, way with her cubs. When handling her young, the mother lioness always kept her razor-sharp claws sheathed in soft paws.

Like most male lions, Koru rarely hunted. He left that up to Mara, for it was she who led the older lionesses on the nightly hunts for food. Jambi respected Mara's skills as a huntress. She was a swift, clever animal who kept the pride well fed.

For a long time, Jambi had been fascinated with the lions. The boy never tired of watching these majestic creatures wander the grasslands in their tawny golden coats. He called the pride the "royal family of the savannah," for wherever the lions walked, all other animals moved out of the way.

Jambi secretly wished he were a member of the pride for, in his own mind, he had formed a special kinship with the lions. He wanted to join them as they rested in the shade of the tree. He longed to pet the cubs and romp with them in the grass. And he wanted to go with Mara and the others on their exciting hunts.

At night Jambi often dreamed he was running across the savannah with the pride. In his sleep, he would see himself run down into the valley with Pika and Kari close behind. Together, he and the cubs would race across the land. Mara would soon appear, gliding gracefully along beside them. Then Meta and Kiwi would dash into sight, and finally Koru would stand up and shake his mane proudly. With a tremendous surge of strength, he would spring forward and pass the others with astounding speed.

Whenever Jambi had this wonderful dream, he, too, was like a lion — swift of foot and strong of heart. The pride never seemed to notice that the boy was different from them. They accepted him as one of the pride.

Sometimes Jambi tried to tell the villagers about the lions, but they did not want to hear about the animals. His parents weren't interested either.

"No more talk about lions!" his mother would say sternly. "Lions and people are not friends."

"You stay away from those lions!" his father would order.

"But they are so beautiful," Jambi tried to explain.

"You will not think they are so beautiful if they decide to have you for dinner!" his mother often warned him.

At such times Jambi would shrug his shoulders and heave a sigh. He knew his parents were concerned for his safety. And he knew lions were dangerous and sometimes attacked humans. But Jambi believed this happened only when people came into the savannah and threatened to hurt the lions.

The boy was convinced that the lions would never harm him. "They know I am almost one of them," he kept telling himself. So each day when no one was looking, Jambi would slip out of the village and go to the savannah.

As the weeks passed, Jambi watched Kari and Pika grow bigger. Now the cubs were making playful attempts to catch small animals. Jambi knew they were developing the hunting skills they would need in order to survive when they were full grown.

Jambi was happy the lions could protect themselves from predators. He knew the only animal the pride had cause to fear was Man. But he also knew there were laws that forbid the hunting of wildlife in this part of the savannah. So Koru and his pride were safe...or so Jambi thought.

One morning as dawn broke over the horizon, the mechanical growl of trucks invaded the peaceful savannah.

"We've got to be quick," said the driver of the lead truck. "We don't want anyone to see us."

"Do not worry," a native scout replied. "Game wardens rarely patrol this area."

"How much farther do we have to go?" the driver asked.

"We are here," the scout answered. "The lions are straight ahead of us."

The trucks rolled to a stop. Three men and the scout grabbed their rifles and jumped to the ground. The lions stirred restlessly. Koru stood up and growled angrily when the three poachers raised their rifles and looked through the telescopic sights.

"I've got the male lion in my sight," one man said.

"I've got a female on target," another spoke out.

"Nigel, you get that cub," the first man ordered.

"Got it!" Nigel grinned.

Three shots rang out. A drug-filled syringe punctured Koru's shoulder, and he stumbled and fell backward. Mara howled with pain when a dart hit her, and Kari was knocked off her feet by the impact of Nigel's shot. As the tranquilizers began to take effect, the lions became drowsy and fell to the ground.

The two old lionesses were not hit, and they quickly fled across the valley. But Pika was so frightened and confused, he didn't know what to do. So he dropped down and tried to hide in the tall grass.

"Look, there's another cub!" the scout shouted.

One of the poachers fired his gun. The dart narrowly missed Pika. Before the man could shoot again, the startled cub sprang to its feet and ran away.

As soon as the lions were unconscious, the poachers drove their trucks close to where the animals lay. The four men struggled to lift Koru's five-hundred-pound body into a cage in the back of the first truck. Mara and her cub were placed in a cage in another truck.

"Let's get out of here!" one of the men yelled.

The poachers quickly climbed into their trucks, started the motors, and drove away.

That afternoon Jambi entered the savannah and looked out over the wide grassland. He noticed the animals were unusually nervous. And when he couldn't see the lions anywhere, the boy's feeling of uneasiness turned into alarm. He hurried back to the village.

"Father, come quickly!" he called. "Something is wrong!"

"What is the matter?" Jono asked.

"The lions are gone!" exclaimed Jambi. "Help me find out what has happened to them."

Jono picked up his spear and followed his son to the savannah. When they found the tire tracks, Jambi's father knelt in the grass and carefully studied the ground. The boy admired the way his father could "read" the signs in the earth.

"Three trucks have been here," Jono said, "and there were four men."

"Did the men kill the lions?" Jambi asked fearfully.

Jono picked up an empty syringe and showed it to his son.

"The lions were not killed," he said. "They were drugged and then taken away in the trucks."

"Were all the lions taken?" Jambi asked anxiously.

"I don't believe so. Some may have escaped. I see the tracks of two adult lions leading off into the grass."

"Who would have done this terrible thing?" Jambi wondered.

"Poachers," Jono told him. "They capture lions and sell them for much money."

Jambi was puzzled. "But, why?" he asked. "People don't eat lions."

"I am told the lions are taken to far-off lands and kept in cages for people to look at," Jono replied.

"That is a cruel thing to do!" Jambi said angrily. "The lions would not be happy living in cages."

"There are laws to protect animals from poachers, but some men do not obey those laws," his father explained sadly.

"Father, let's get all the men in our village and go free the lions!" urged Jambi.

"Don't speak such nonsense," his father replied. "Our spears are no match for the poachers' guns."

A rustling of leaves caught Jono's attention. He turned and saw a cub peek its head out from behind a bush.

"There is one of the cubs," Jono said, pointing to the young lion.

"It's Pika!" Jambi exclaimed. "The poachers did not get him!"

"So I see," Jono said. "Now come, we must return to the village."

"But, Father, we can't leave the cub here alone! He has never hunted and made his first kill. Pika will starve if we leave him to find food on his own."

"It is not our place to interfere with the ways of nature," Jono replied. "If it is meant for the cub to survive, he will survive."

"But, Father..." Jambi began to plead.

"Enough!" Jono said sternly. "Come, we must leave at once."

Jambi had no choice but to follow his father. As they walked away, the boy looked over his shoulder at Pika. The cub was standing all alone by the acacia tree.

For the rest of the day and into the evening, Jambi worried about Pika. He was sure Mara was one of the captured lions, for she never would have run off and deserted her cub. Finally, that night as his parents slept, the boy crept out of their hut. Taking a spear and a chunk of smoked meat with him, he hurried to the savannah.

Jambi had no trouble finding the cub. Pika was still by the tree. It seemed as if he had been waiting for Jambi. When the boy threw a piece of the meat to Pika, the cub quickly gobbled it down. Then he looked toward Jambi for more. With every piece the boy tossed, he edged closer to the lion. At last, Jambi was so near to the cub that Pika took the last bit of food from the boy's hand.

After the cub had eaten, he lay down and purred contentedly. Jambi sat down beside his new friend, then cautiously reached over and gently placed his hand on top of Pika's head. The cub did not seem to mind being touched, so the boy began to pet him. Pika started purring even louder, and soon he was asleep.

Jambi leaned back against the tree, but he could not sleep. The sounds of animals moving about on the savannah made him feel uneasy. Jambi knew if any of the lions returned, they might not be as friendly as Pika. So he stayed awake all night, listening, watching, and thinking.

Jambi realized he could not feed the cub every day. His parents would not allow that. He also knew he could not stand by and let Pika starve. So toward morning he decided there was only one thing to do. He must find the poachers and set the lions free. The boy didn't know if he could do that alone, but he knew he had to try.

PROPERTY OF
ELMWOOD SCHOOLS
RHINELAND SCHOOL DIVISION #18

After sunrise Jambi tip-toed away from the sleeping cub and began following the tire tracks. He had walked only a mile across the savannah when he heard a sound behind him. With his heart pounding, he spun around and raised his spear. It was Pika. Jambi laughed with relief. At the same time, he was worried because the cub had not stayed by the tree.

"Go back, Pika!" he shouted and clapped his hands. "It isn't safe for you to come with me."

But Pika did not understand. He just kept rolling over and over in the grass, wanting to play.

"Oh, all right, Pika," Jambi finally gave in. "I guess you can come along with me."

As Jambi walked ahead, Pika followed, jumping playfully at the boy's heels. By noon the hot African sun poured down on them. Jambi and Pika stopped by a shallow stream for a drink of water. Then the boy stood up and waded across to the other side. But Pika stayed at the water's edge and paced nervously back and forth.

"Don't be afraid of the water, Pika. Come on across," Jambi urged.

Pika still did not like the idea. He sat down and meowed loudly.

"If you don't come with me now, I will have to go on without you," the boy said. Then he turned to leave.

Not wanting to be left alone, the cub splashed into the water, waded across the stream, and bounded ashore. Jambi laughed as he watched Pika toss his golden head and shake the water from his fur.

The boy began looking for tire tracks on the shore, but he could find none. The poachers must have kept their trucks in the water and driven them along the streambed. But did they go upstream or downstream? Jambi had no way of knowing. He decided to search upstream.

"Come on, Pika," he called.

But Pika refused to follow. The cub kept growling and sniffing the grass that grew near the water. He clearly wanted to go downstream. Jambi decided Pika was probably right because the cub was a wild animal with a keen sense of smell. So the boy shrugged his shoulders and followed Pika's lead.

They had not walked very far before Jambi saw ruts in the muddy bank where the trucks had pulled out of the stream. He and the cub followed the tire tracks all afternoon.

In the evening they reached the top of a hill. Jambi quickly stopped and dropped to the ground. The poachers' camp was in sight! The boy cautiously raised his head and peeked over the crest of the slope. He began to tremble with more fear and excitement than he had ever known. Pika crept up beside him and started sniffing the air. Jambi supposed the cub was smelling the scent of the captured lions.

But Pika had noticed something else. A guinea hen was moving in the tall grass. The cub rose to his feet and quietly stalked his prey. When he was only a few feet away, the hen saw him and began to squawk. She flapped her wings and started to take flight. It was too late. Pika pounced on the hen and grabbed her between his teeth.

Jambi was thrilled to see Pika make his first kill! He knew the cub now had a chance to survive on its own.

Pika proudly carried the dead bird to Jambi and dropped it at the boy's feet. The cub was willing to share the food.

Although Jambi did not like the taste of raw meat, he dared not start a fire so close to the poachers' camp. But he was so hungry, he knew he had to have something to eat. So, like wild brothers, the boy and the lion ate the raw meat together.

After they had eaten, Pika fell asleep. This pleased Jambi because he did not want the cub to go with him to the camp. As soon as it was dark, Jambi took his spear and quietly made his way down the hill. Before long he was close enough to the camp to hear the men talking.

"If we get a cheetah tonight, we'll leave here," one man said.

"That's fine with me," answered another. "A cheetah and three lions will sell for big money."

Jambi crept closer and peered through the tall grass. He saw two poachers and a scout walk away from the small campfire and climb into one of the trucks. A fourth man stood near two cages that were covered with large canvas tarps.

"Nigel," the driver of the truck said, "you stay here and guard the camp. And don't put anymore logs on the fire. You don't want to attract the attention of the game wardens."

"But it gets cold at night," complained Nigel.

"Then put on your jacket!" the driver replied gruffly.

The engine was started, and the truck rumbled across the shadowy grassland and disappeared into the darkness. Then Jambi heard a lion's roar.

"Shut up, you noisy animal!" Nigel yelled as he slipped into his jacket. Then he walked over and stretched out beside the fire.

Jambi knew the sound of Koru's roar. After the poacher had fallen asleep, the boy stole quietly past him to the cages. When he untied the canvas coverings and peeked under them, the lions began to stir restlessly.

"Shhhhh!" Jambi said, trying to keep them quiet.

It didn't help. Koru hit against the side of his cage and let out a mighty roar. Mara hissed and snarled at Jambi, while Kari tried to hide behind her mother.

"What's going on over there?" Nigel yelled, jumping to his feet. "Hey, Boy, what are you doing around those cages?"

Nigel grabbed his rifle and ran toward Jambi. The boy quickly forced the metal pin from the lock on Koru's cage. Then he flung the door wide open and stepped back.

Koru leaped out and jumped on Nigel, knocking the man down. As the poacher hit the ground, his rifle went off, and he dropped the gun. The loud noise startled the lioness and her cub. As soon as Jambi unlocked the door to their cage, they bolted to freedom too.

Nigel tried to get up, but Koru lunged and knocked him down again. The angry lion circled the poacher and growled ferociously. When he jumped on top of Nigel and pinned him down, the man screamed for help.

Jambi dashed to the campfire and grabbed a burning stick from the embers. Then he scurried from tent to tent, setting each one on fire. He hoped the blaze would be seen by the game wardens.

When Koru saw the fire, he fled into the darkness. Nigel staggered to his feet and picked up his rifle. He yelled at Jambi, then aimed the gun and fired. The bullet barely missed the boy's shoulder.

Jambi didn't wait for another shot. The frightened boy ran away as fast as he could. Nigel aimed his rifle again, but before he could pull the trigger, an explosion hurled him across the ground. The fire had reached some drums of gasoline that were stacked near the tents.

The boy turned and watched in amazement as the fierce blaze lighted up the night sky. He was relieved to see that Nigel was not following him.

Jambi hurried on up the hill. When he reached the top, he turned again and saw the headlights of two trucks that were closing in on the camp. The trucks stopped and two men climbed out. Jambi smiled when he saw them grab Nigel and handcuff him. The boy knew the men must be game wardens. He hoped they would find all the poachers and put them in jail.

Jambi could not see the lions anywhere. He knew he might never see them again. But the important thing was that he had set them free. Now he must find Pika and return home.

Jambi called out the cub's name over and over and frantically searched the area for his friend. The cub did not appear. Finally, Jambi realized that Pika was gone too. He hoped the cub was safe with Mara and the other lions.

Jambi was tired and sleepy, but he knew he must return to the village immediately. So he walked off into the night, facing the long journey home alone.

Early in the morning, Jambi came to the stream and saw his father standing on the far bank. The boy knew he was in trouble for disobeying Jono. He slowly waded across the water and stood quietly before his father.

"Where have you been?" his father asked sternly.

Jambi told him how he had tracked the poachers to their camp and set the lions free from the cages.

"I see," said Jono. "But why did the sky glow so brightly last night?" he asked.

"I set the poachers' tents on fire."

"That was a dangerous thing for you to do," his father said. "Your mother and I have been very worried about you."

"I'm sorry," Jambi apologized.

"I am very disappointed in you because you did not obey me," his father scolded. "But I am also very proud to have such a brave son. Come, Jambi, we must return to the village. Your mother is waiting."

During the following months, Jambi often walked to the savannah, hoping to see that Koru and his pride had returned. But there was no sign of them.

Then, one morning as Jambi looked out over the valley, he was filled with joy. By the acacia tree stood Koru. The two old lionesses were there, too, sleeping peacefully, and Kari was rolling in the grass. But, where were Pika and his mother? What had happened to them? he wondered.

Hearing a slight sound behind him, Jambi turned quickly and looked. There was Pika, standing only a few feet away. And Mara was nearby, guarding her cub.

The boy wanted to rush to Pika and pet him. But with Mara so close, Jambi knew better than to do such a thing. So he stood absolutely still, aware of Mara's alert eyes watching him.

Pika was delighted to see Jambi too. The cub jumped forward eagerly and started to run to the boy. A warning growl from Mara stopped Pika in his tracks.

For a few moments, the boy, the cub, and the lioness looked at each other. Then Mara growled again, and Pika obediently went to stand beside his mother.

Jambi watched as the cub followed Mara across the savannah to join the pride. Only once did Pika hesitate and turn to look at Jambi. Then the cub turned back and walked away.

The sight of the lions gathered at the acacia tree pleased the boy. Now the savannah looked whole and complete.

Aruna Chandrasekhar
age 9

Anika Thomas
age 13

Cara Reichel
age 15

Jonathan Kahn
age 9

Adam Moore
age 9

Leslie Ann MacKeen
age 9

Elizabeth Haidle
age 13

Amy Hagstrom
age 9

Isaac Whitlatch
age 11

Dav Pilkey
age 19

OLIVER and the OIL SPILL
written and illustrated by ARUNA CHANDRASEKHAR

by Aruna Chandrasekhar, age 9
Houston, Texas
A touching and timely story! When the lives of many otters are threatened by a huge oil spill, a group of concerned people come to their rescue. Wonderful illustrations.
Printed Full Color
ISBN 0-933849-33-8

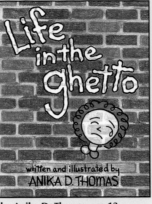

Life in the ghetto
written and illustrated by ANIKA D. THOMAS

by Anika D. Thomas, age 13
Pittsburgh, Pennsylvania
A compelling autobiography! A young girl's heartrending account of growing up in a tough, inner-city neighborhood. The illustrations match the mood of this gripping story.
Printed Two Colors
ISBN 0-933849-34-6

A STONE PROMISE BY CARA REICHEL

by Cara Reichel, age 15
Rome, Georgia
Elegant and eloquent! A young stonecutter vows to create a great statue for his impoverished village. But his fame almost stops him from fulfilling that promise.
Printed Two Colors
ISBN 0-933849-35-4

PATULOU THE PRAIRIE RATTLESNA
written and illustrated by JONATHAN KAHN

by Jonathan Kahn, age 9
Richmond Heights, Ohio
A fascinating nature story! Patulous, a prairie rattle searches for food, he must avoid the claws and fangs of h enemies.
Printed Full Color
ISBN 0-933849-36-2

BROKEN ARROW BOY
WRITTEN AND ILLUSTRATED BY ADAM MOORE and his friends

by Adam Moore, age 9
Broken Arrow, Oklahoma
A remarkable true story! When Adam was eight years old, he fell and ran an arrow into his head. With rare insight and humor, he tells of his ordeal and his amazing recovery.
Printed Two Colors
ISBN 0-933849-24-9

GET THAT GOAT!
WRITTEN AND ILLUSTRATED BY MICHAEL AUSHENKER

by Michael Aushenker, age 19
Ithaca, New York
Chomp! Chomp! When Arthur forgets to feed his goat, the animal eats everything in sight. A very funny story — good to the last bite. The illustrations are terrific.
Printed Full Color
ISBN 0-933849-28-1

WHO CAN FIX IT?
written & illustrated by Leslie Ann MacKeen

by Leslie Ann MacKeen, age 9
Winston-Salem, North Carolina
Loaded with fun and puns! When Jeremiah T. Fitz's car stops running, several animals offer suggestions for fixing it. The results are hilarious. The illustrations are charming.
Printed Full Color
ISBN 0-933849-19-2

ELMER the GRUMP
written and illustrated by ELIZABETH HAIDLE

by Elizabeth Haidle, age 13
Beaverton, Oregon
A very touching story! The g iest Elfkin learns to cheri friendship of others after he an injured snail and befrien orphaned boy. Absolutely be
Printed Full Color
ISBN 0-933849-20-6

Strong and free
written and illustrated by Amy Hagstrom

by Amy Hagstrom, age 9
Portola, California
An exciting western! When a boy and an old Indian try to save a herd of wild ponies, they discover a lost canyon and see the mystical vision of the Great White Stallion.
Printed Full Color
ISBN 0-933849-15-X

ME AND MY VEGGIES

by Isaac Whitlatch, age 11
Casper, Wyoming
The true confessions of a devout vegetable hater! Isaac tells ways to avoid and dispose of the "slimy green things." His colorful illustrations provide a salad of laughter and mirth.
Printed Full Color
ISBN 0-933849-16-8

WORLD WAR WON
written & illustrated by Dav Pilkey

by Dav Pilkey, age 19
Cleveland, Ohio
A thought-provoking parable! Two kings halt an arms race and learn to live in peace. This outstanding book launched Dav's career. He now has seven more books published.
Printed Full Color
ISBN 0-933849-22-2

Walking is Wild Weird and Wacky
written and illustrated by Karen Kerber

by Karen Kerber, age 12
St. Louis, Missouri
A delightfully playful book! is loaded with clever alliterati gentle humor. Karen's brigh ored illustrations are compo wiggly and waggly strokes of
Printed Full Color
ISBN 0-933849-29-X

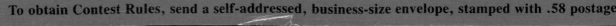

To obtain Contest Rules, send a self-addressed, business-size envelope, stamped with .58 postage